The Little Fir Tree
El Pequeñito Pino

by

Dr. Jane J. Jenkins

Illustrations by L.S. Wefel and Janet Grenda

Dr. Jane J. Jenkins is a master storyteller, mother, grandmother, and great grandmother who lives in Aspen, Colorado, with her husband Jim. In the 1970s Dr. Jane created the PBS series *The Magic Teapot*. Dr. Jane collaborated with artist Janet Grenda on *The Adventures of Harry the Hamster* in 2001 and, in 2009, *The Further Adventures of Harry the Hamster*.

The Little Fir Tree is a true story written for children with special needs. The tree, located in Aspen, was measured in 1985 at 61 feet. In 2006, it was 91 feet. It is estimated that at the time this book went to press in 2011, the Little Fir Tree was approximately 95 feet tall.

Each year on the first Sunday of December, the decorated tree is lit up in a town-wide celebration launching the holiday season in Aspen, Colorado. This book honors the Little Fir Tree's spirit of survival.

ISBN: 978-0-9847972-1-9

© copyright 2011, by Jane J. Jenkins

CPSIA Compliance Information: Batch #1111. For further information contact RJ Communications, NY NY, 800-621-2556.

The Little Fir Tree was first published in English and © copyright 1976 by the Aspen Historical Society, Aspen, Colorado.

El Pequeñito Pino was first published in Spanish and © copyright 1976 by the Aspen Historical Society, Aspen, Colorado.

A full-color edition in English was re-published as *The Little Fir Tree* and © copyright 2005 by Jane Jenkins.

The present edition is the first bilingual edition.

AGS Publishing
dba Aspen Graphic Solutions, Inc.
391 Boundary Lane · Carbondale, CO 81623

Book management, design and production by Aspen Graphic Solutions, Inc., Marjorie DeLuca, designer.

Manufactured in U.S.A.

The Little Fir Tree
is dedicated to all
the special children
in the world.

This story was inspired by
Mauri Jenkins,
who is
God's special child.

Once there was an ugly stunted little fir tree. It had been that way for a long, long time.

When Dr. Twining sold his lovely home to Mr. and Mrs. Sardy and their two children, he said:

"I think you will like your new home. All these trees in the front yard are healthy and sturdy, except that ugly one in the corner.

"I think you ought to chop it down."

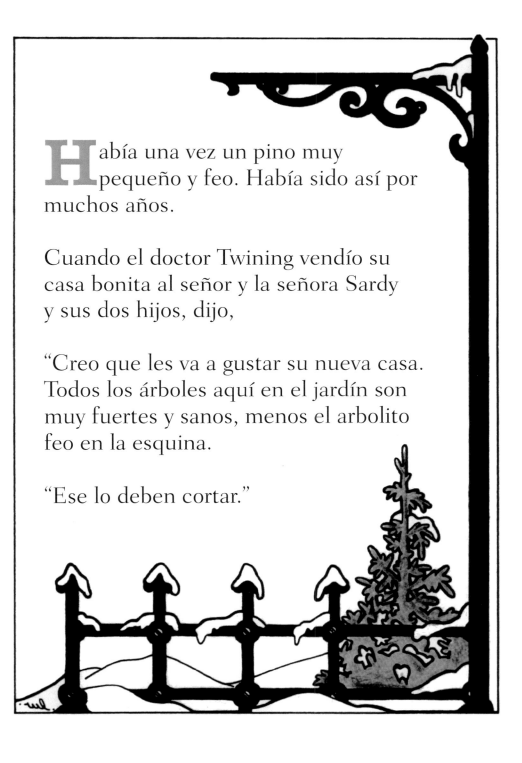

Había una vez un pino muy
pequeño y feo. Había sido así por
muchos años.

Cuando el doctor Twining vendío su
casa bonita al señor y la señora Sardy
y sus dos hijos, dijo,

"Creo que les va a gustar su nueva casa.
Todos los árboles aquí en el jardín son
muy fuertes y sanos, menos el arbolito
feo en la esquina.

"Ese lo deben cortar."

The children, T.J. and Sylvia, said, "Oh, please don't cut it down, Daddy. It is just our size! Let's see if we can help it grow."

So it was decided to let the ugly little tree go through one more winter.

The poor little fir tree with her stiff, green needles stood right against the dust and dirt of the cold fall winds.

Each day Mr. Sardy and the children hosed the dust and dirt from the branches of trees in the front yard.

Los niños, el T.J. y la Sylvia, dijeron "¡Ay papá! Por favor, no lo corte. ¡Es exactamente de tamaño nuestro! A ver si no lo podemos ayudar a crecer."

Entonces decidieron no cortar el pinito feo hasta la próxima primavera.

El pobre pino con sus ramitas verdes se plantó allí contra el polvo y el viento frío del otoño.

Cada día el señor Sardy y los niños quitaban el polvo de las ramas de los árboles en el jardín del frente.

Now, the Little Fir Tree thought that she was ugly because she had watched the gentle, swaying aspen trees turn from a pure emerald green in the spring to a soft golden yellow in the fall.

The Little Fir Tree listened to the lullabies that the wind played on their delicate, fragile branches.

El pequeño pino se pensaba muy feo. Había mirado las hojas de los otros árboles cambiar de verde a un amarillo brillante a lo largo del otoño.

El pinito escuchaba la música del viento pasando por sus ramas frágiles y delicadas.

The Little Fir Tree told the cold North Wind of her unhappiness in being stunted and ugly.

El pequeñito pino le contaba al viento frío del norte su tristeza a causa de ser tan feo y pequeño.

One day two little birds who loved to perch in the Fir Tree's branches and the long-eared jackrabbits that ran through the grass heard the poor Little Fir Tree crying.

Un día dos pajaritos a quienes les gustaba sentarse en las ramas del arbolito y los conejos de orejas largas que brincaban por el pasto escucharon el pobrecito pino llorando.

All day the little birds flew around Aspen looking for food and they thought about their friend who had given them warmth and comfort…

Todo el día los pajaritos volaban por la cuidad de Aspen buscando comida y pensaban en su amigo, el pinito, que les había dado tanta hospitalidad y cariño…

…against the
cold, icy blasts of
the Colorado winter.

…contra el viento frío y
helado del invierno
de Colorado.

One day the mother bird was searching the streets for a bit of breakfast and she spied some golden shavings from the portico of the famous Red Onion.

"I wonder," she said, "if the Little Fir Tree would like this lovely bit of gold to wear on one of her branches.

"I think I'll take it to her."
And she did.

Un día la pajarita madre estaba buscando en las calles por un pedacito de comida y vió un trozo de pintura dorada en la entrada del famoso restaurante, La Cebolla Roja.

"Sea que al pinito la gustaría este pedacito de oro para sus ramas," dijo ella.

"Se lo llevaré."
Y se lo llevó.

The gold shavings glittered in the bright
sun and the Little Fir Tree thought,
"How beautiful." And she smiled just a little.

The next day the father bird found
a piece of beautiful blue glass that had
fallen from the stained glass windows
of the Crystal Palace. He took it back
to the Little Fir Tree.

He hung it on the opposite side from the
lovely golden shavings.

Los pedacitos de oro brillaban en la
luz del sol, y el pequeñito pino
pensó, "¡Ay! ¡Que bello!"
Y le salió una sonrisa pequeñita.

El próximo día el padre de los pájaros
encontró un pedazo de cristal azul que
había caído de la ventana del
Palacio de Cristales. Se lo llevó al pinito.

Colgó el cristal al otro lado de
los pedacitos de oro.

The bit
of bright
blue glass
caught the
warmth of the
winter sunlight
and cast a
rainbow
of shining colors
on the deep snow.

The golden shavings
became a burnished amber
in the late afternoon sun.

El trozo
de cristal
captó la luz
del sol
y echó
un bello arcoiris
sobre la nieve
blanca y pura.

Los pedacitos de oro
brillaban
en la luz ambarina
de la tarde.

"Oh, my goodness,"
said the Little Fir Tree.
"How beautiful that is,"
and she rustled her branches
holding the bit of
bright blue glass
and she felt
just a little bit better.

In fact,
she almost felt beautiful.

"Dios mío!"
dijo el árbolito.
"¡Qué bonito estoy!"
y estiró sus ramas,
sosteniendo
el trozo de cristal,
y se sintió
un poquito mejor.

Por ese momento,
se sintió bello.

Each day the little birds found something lovely with which to decorate the Little Fir Tree.

One day they brought a bit of lace from a curtain in the window of the Hotel Jerome.

Another day they found a string of popcorn from the Popcorn Wagon.

A fat red and white candy cane from the Peppermint Tree was a special treat.

Cada día los pajaritos encontraron algo bello con que adornar el pinito.

Un día trajeron un pedacito de encaje de una cortina en la ventaña del Hotel Jerome.

Otro día encontraron una cuerdecilla de palomitas del vendedor de palomitas en la esquina.

Una dulce del Peppermint Tree fue una sorpresa especial.

Just before Christmas,
a delivery boy
from the bakery
dropped a box of
fat little gingerbread men,
and the two little birds
struggled with
one little man
that was
forgotten in the snow.

Pocos días antes de la Navidad,
el chico
de la panaderia
trajo una caja de pan
de jengibre hecho
a forma de hombre.
Los pájaros recogíeron
un hombrecito jengibre
que se había olvidado
en la nieve.

Gradually the Little Fir Tree was decorated with the treasures that the birds had found abandoned in the nooks and crannies of the town. Each day the Little Fir Tree changed just a little.

No longer did she feel ugly and stunted. She began to unbend a little and to grow and to think beautiful thoughts about herself.

She began to smile and be happy and enjoy her new-found beauty. She began to glow from the care and concern that the little birds had given her.

Poco a poco el pequeñito pino fue decorado con los tesoros abandonados que traían los pajaritos. Cada día el pinito cambiaba.

Ya no se sentía féo. Empezó a estirar sus ramas y crecer y pensar cosas bellas sobre sí mismo.

Empezó a sonreír y estar feliz y disfrutar su nueva belleza a causa de todo el cariño que le habían dado los pajaritos.

As Christmastime approached, the Sardy family began to make preparations for the holiday season.

Sylvia and T.J. said, "Dad, may we decorate the trees in the front yard?"

"I guess so," said their Dad, thinking about the extra work that it would be.

The children and their father went out into the front yard to make their plans.

Por la Navidad, la familia Sardy empezó a hacer las preparaciones festivas.

Sylvia y T.J. pidieron, "Papá, ¿podemos decorar los árboles en el jardín?"

"Bueno, hijos, si quieren," les dijo su padre, pensando en todo el trabajo que esto le costaría.

Los hijos y el padre salieron al jardín para hacer sus planes.

Sylvia said, "Oh look, Dad, how beautiful the Little Fir Tree is!" Her brother said, "Why, the tree is covered with bright decorations."

"Well," said Mr. Sardy, "I don't know who has decorated the little tree, but she is beautiful. I think that I will put Christmas lights on these trees each year so that everyone can enjoy our beautiful garden."

Sylvia dijo, "¡Mira papá, que bello está el arbolito pino!" Su hermano dijo, "Está cubierto de adornos brilliantes."

"Pues," dijo el señor Sardy, "no sé quien haya decorado este arbolito, pero está bellísimo. Creo que pondré luces bonitas en todos estos árboles cada año para que todos podrán disfrutar de nuestro bello jardín."

So each year Mr. Sardy and the children would decorate the trees in their front yard with colored lights to officially start the Christmas season.

Today you can still see the Little Fir Tree in the corner of Sardy's front yard.

No longer is she ugly and stunted, but she is tall and beautiful. In fact, she is the tallest tree in Aspen, and as she stands majestically in the snow, she seems to smile her welcome to all that come to Aspen, Colorado.

Entonces cada año el padre y los hijos decoraban todos los árboles del jardín con luces de todos colores para dar la bienvenida a la Navidad.

Hoy día todavía se puede ver el pino en la esquina de su jardín.

Ya no es ni feo ni pequeño, sino que alto y bello. Ahora es el árbol más alto de toda la cuidad. Parado majestuosamente en la nieve, sonríe su bienvenida a todos que vienen a Aspen, Colorado.

THE END

FIN